28/03/2017

Penelope
the Foal
Fairy

Join the **Rainbow Magic Reading Challenge!**

Read the story and collect your fairy points to climb the

To Rowena, who loves foals

Special thanks to
Rachel Elliot

ORCHARD BOOKS

First published in Great Britain in 2017 by The Watts Publishing Group

1 3 5 7 9 10 8 6 4 2

© 2017 Rainbow Magic Limited.
© 2017 HIT Entertainment Limited.
Illustrations © Orchard Books 2017

HiT entertainment

A CIP catalogue record for this book is available from the British Library.

ISBN 978 1 40834 516 0

Printed and bound in Great Britain by CPI Group (UK) Ltd, Croydon, CR0 4YY

MIX
Paper from
responsible sources
FSC® C104740
www.fsc.org

The paper and board used in this book are made from wood from responsible sources.

Orchard Books
An imprint of Hachette Children's Group
Part of The Watts Publishing Group Limited
Carmelite House, 50 Victoria Embankment, London EC4Y 0DZ

An Hachette UK Company
www.hachette.co.uk
www.hachettechildrens.co.uk

Penelope
the Foal
Fairy

by Daisy Meadows

ORCHARD

www.rainbowmagic.co.uk

Jack Frost's Spell

I want a farm that's just for me,
With animals I won't set free.
It's far too slow to seek each one.
Let fairy magic get this done!

With magic from the fairy farm,
I'll grant my wish – to their alarm!
And if I spoil the humans' fun,
Then Jack Frost really will have won!

Contents

Chapter One: Poster Animals   9

Chapter Two: A Muddy Mess   21

Chapter Three: Jack Frost's Pets   31

Chapter Four: Sad Snow Geese   41

Chapter Five: A Spell and a Splash   53

Chapter Six: True Friends   65

Poster Animals

"Just one day left until the farm's grand opening," said Kirsty Tate.

She was peering at a computer screen over the shoulders of Harriet and Niall Hawkins, the owners of Greenfields Farm. Her parents, Mr and Mrs Tate, and her best friend, Rachel Walker, were also gazing at the computer. They were all looking at the design for the new poster to advertise the farm.

"I feel jumpy with excitement every time I think about the grand opening tomorrow," said Rachel.

"I feel jumpy with *nervousness* every time I think about it," said Harriet with a laugh. "I can't believe there's just one day left."

"I'm sure everything will be fine," said Mr Tate, patting Harriet's shoulder.

The Tates and Rachel were all spending spring half term at Greenfields Farm, just outside Wetherbury. The Tates were friends with Harriet and Niall, and they had all been helping to get the farm ready. Tomorrow, Greenfields Farm would open to visitors for the first time, complete with a children's petting farm.

"You've all been wonderful," said Niall, half turning in his chair to smile up at them. "Especially you, Rachel and Kirsty. We were worried about being too busy to look after the baby animals this week, but you've done everything for them."

"It's been a treat to look after them," said Kirsty with a smile.

Mr Tate was still gazing at the poster design.

"I think it needs more photos of the farm," he said.

"How about adding some photos of the baby animals?" said Rachel. "They are so cute – they'd make anyone want to visit the farm."

"Especially animal lovers like us," Kirsty added.

"We could add some photos of the foals," said Harriet. "They're really sweet – especially when they've just been groomed and are all nice and clean."

"I saw them this morning and they are definitely not clean at the moment," said Niall with a chuckle. "I'd never seen such scruffy-looking foals before. Girls,  would you mind bathing and grooming the foals before they have their photo taken?"

Rachel and Kirsty exchanged a glance of pure delight.

"Bathing foals sounds like so much fun," said Rachel. "We'd love to do that."

"You'll need to put on your wellies and your oldest clothes," said Harriet. "I've found that the animals end up clean but the people bathing them certainly don't."

Shortly afterwards, the best friends were walking towards the stables, with two buckets of hot soapy water and the grooming equipment. They were wearing fraying old T-shirts and threadbare jeans, and they couldn't stop smiling.

"I think we're going to need every drop of this water," said Kirsty. "We must get the foals lovely and neat so that they look good for the posters."

"The foals are adorable, even if they are muddy," said Kirsty. "And they make such happy little neighing noises."

"Look, there's Blossom," said Rachel, spotting the cow outside her barn. "Let's go and say hello."

They hurried over, stopping to pick some juicy green grass for Blossom. She munched on it and then gave them a friendly moo.

"We're going to bath and groom the foals," Kirsty told her. "Wish us luck."

Blossom gave an extra-loud moo, which made the girls laugh. They said goodbye and then carried on along the lane towards the stables. It was another sunny morning on the farm, and the air was filled with the sounds of animals all around, and the high, clear twitter of the birds.

"Everyone seems to be happy that it's springtime," said Rachel.

"*I'm* happy that it's the spring holiday, and

16

we're spending it together," Kirsty replied, smiling at her best friend.

The girls had shared many adventures, but they never grew tired of being together. They always had lots of fun. Best of all, they had a very exciting secret, which they had never told anyone else. They were friends of Fairyland, and had met lots of fairies since they first met on Rainspell Island.

"Look," said Rachel as they passed the horses' paddock. "I think the horses are watching something over by the pigsty. I wonder what it could be."

Four of the horses were standing in a line with their backs to the girls. It was hard to see around them, and the girls climbed up on to the paddock gate, but they still couldn't see over their heads.

"Let's go and check if everything's OK," said Kirsty. "If there's something wrong, we'll have to run back and tell Niall and Harriet."

They put down their buckets and brushes, and then climbed over the gate and dropped into the grassy paddock.

The horses took no notice, even when the girls came to stand beside them. Then Rachel and Kirsty saw what they were looking at.

"Oh my goodness," said Kirsty. "The foals have got into the pigs' enclosure!"

"That's not all," said Rachel. "Just look at what they're *doing*!"

A Muddy Mess

There was plenty of mud around the
pigsty. It was exactly the sort of squishy
mud that piglets love. But there wasn't
a single piglet to be seen. Instead, three
little foals with fluffy coats and long
manes were rolling around in the mud.
The girls looked around and saw another
foal jumping into a big muddy puddle

with a splash. As
they watched,
it threw
back its
head and
let out
a loud
oinking
sound.

The horses in the
paddock took a few steps backwards, and
the girls exchanged a worried glance.

"The foals are acting like piglets," said
Kirsty. "Oh, Rachel, we know what this
means."

"Yes," said Rachel, looking serious. "It
means more trouble from Jack Frost and
his naughty goblins."

On the day they arrived at Greenfields

Farm, Kirsty and Rachel had met
Debbie the Duckling Fairy. She had
whisked them to the Fluttering Fairyland
Farm, a magical farm hovering among
the puffy white clouds over Fairyland.

Debbie had introduced the girls to

the other Baby Farm Animal Fairies
and their magical baby farm animals
– Splashy the duckling, Fluffy the lamb,
Frisky the foal and Chompy the baby
goat. The girls had been delighted to
find out that the magical animals helped
the Baby Farm Animal Fairies to look
after baby farm animals everywhere.

But as the girls were walking around
Fluttering Fairyland Farm with the
fairies and Farmer Francis, Jack Frost
and his goblins had stolen the fairies'
magical farm animals. Jack Frost was
making his own petting farm at his Ice
Castle, and he wanted to fill it with lots
of cute and cuddly farm animals. He
said his pet snow goose and her baby,
Snowdrop, needed friends, so he was
going to use the fairies' magical animals

to get more baby farm animals.

Jack Frost's plan had already caused chaos at Greenfields Farm.

"First the ducklings acted like puppies, and then the lambs behaved like kittens," said Kirsty. "Now the foals are not themselves. What are we going to do?"

Rachel glanced over at the horses again. They looked just as worried as she felt. Then she saw something out of the corner of her eye.

One of the bales of hay that were scattered around the paddock was glowing. Her heart gave a leap of excitement.

"Kirsty!" Rachel said in an eager voice. "I think there's magic happening over there."

The girls hurried over to the hay bale and kneeled down in front of it. The glow grew brighter, and the hay seemed to turn golden. Rachel and Kirsty saw it moving and reached out their hands. At once, Penelope the Foal Fairy fluttered out of the centre, shaking stray bits of hay from her gossamer wings.

She was wearing flowery boots with a matching headscarf, a crisp white shirt and a skirt as blue as the sky.

"Hello, Penelope," said Kirsty. "Have you come to help the foals?"

Penelope glanced over to where the foals were still rolling around in the mud. But then she shook her head.

"I wish I could help them," she said in a soft voice. "But I can't return them to

normal without Frisky. That's why I'm
here. I've found out that Jack Frost has
got Frisky at his Ice Castle. Please, will
you come with me and help me to get
him back?"

Rachel and Kirsty had already helped
Debbie the Duckling Fairy and Elodie
the Lamb Fairy get their magical
animals safely back home to Fluttering
Fairyland Farm. But
there were still
two magical
animals
missing,
and if
they
didn't
come home
very soon,

Greenfields Farm wouldn't be ready to open on time. They knew that the fairies were depending on them.

"Of course we will," said Rachel. "We have to get Frisky back – and quickly!"

Jack Frost's Pets

Penelope gave her wand a little flick, and a shower of pink fairy dust fluttered down around Rachel and Kirsty. They closed their eyes and felt something warm slip around their shoulders as they shrank to fairy size. Their wings unfurled and lifted them into the air. Then a blast of icy wind blew the fairy dust away.

The girls opened their eyes and found that they were flying high above the Ice Castle in Fairyland. Penelope's magic had given each of them a fluffy cape around their shoulders.

"These will keep you warm and cosy, however bitterly cold it gets," said Penelope. "My fairy magic is enough to

keep me warm."

Rachel and Kirsty shivered, feeling glad of the capes. Jack Frost's castle was always a chilly place, but today it seemed colder than ever. There was a grim cloud looming so low that it touched the turrets.

"If Frisky is here, we'll find him," said Kirsty. "Come on, let's fly down and look around."

There were no goblins guarding the grey turrets, so the three fairies zoomed down and perched there to look into a little courtyard garden at the back of the castle. It was decorated with ice statues of animals, but there were some living creatures there too.

"There's the snow goose," said Rachel.

"And baby Snowdrop," Kirsty added.

"And Frisky!" cried Penelope. "Frisky is there too!"

The three fairies shared happy smiles. It was wonderful to see Frisky again. He looked just like the foals at Greenfields Farm, except he had an extra magical sparkle. But their smiles faded when they saw that he was bumbling around the courtyard like a pig. Snowdrop, the baby snow goose, was hopping around after him, honking happily. The snow goose was watching them both with a puzzled expression. She was sitting beside a large, brown sack. It was tied with a white rope and it was labelled 'Snow Goose Treats'.

"Even the snow goose is wondering

why Frisky isn't acting like a foal," said Kirsty.

Snowdrop and Frisky were now chasing each other around the ice statues and trying to pounce on each other. They were clearly having lots of fun.

"There's no sign of Jack Frost or the goblins," Penelope said. "Let's go and get Frisky right now."

She fluttered her wings and started to rise into the air, but Rachel put a hand on her arm to stop her.

"Hold on," she said. "We have to be careful."

As she spoke, Jack Frost hurried out into the courtyard, wearing a pair of bright green dungarees. Penelope sank

down beside Rachel and Kirsty again
and they watched the Ice Lord, their
hearts hammering. A few seconds later
and he would have seen Penelope.

Jack Frost scooped Frisky into his bony
arms and cuddled him tightly. Frisky
wriggled and
writhed, trying to
get away.

"Frisky doesn't
like being
squeezed," said
Penelope.

Clinging on to
the wriggly foal,
Jack Frost bent
down and opened
the sack that the
girls had seen earlier.

He pulled out a handful of something
that looked like birdseed and held it
under Frisky's snout. Frisky gave an oink,
leapt out of Jack Frost's arms and jumped
to the ground. He aimed a hard kick at
the sack of snow goose treats, and then
darted off again.

"Come back!" Jack Frost wailed.

The snow goose and Snowdrop waddled over to the sack and started to nudge it with their beaks, looking up at Jack Frost with hopeful expressions. But Jack Frost shook his head at them and tied up the sack.

"No," he said. "If Frisky doesn't want these, no one is having them."

Sad Snow Geese

The snow geese waddled away, their white heads drooping a little.

"They look so sad," said Rachel.

"Poor things," Penelope said. "They chose to be Jack Frost's special pets. They really love him."

"But why is he ignoring the snow geese?" Kirsty asked.

"He's just really interested in his petting farm now," said Penelope. "He isn't thinking about the geese."

Rachel and Kirsty looked at each other, knowing that they were both thinking the same thing. If they could get Frisky back for Penelope, maybe Jack Frost would again start noticing the geese who loved him so much.

"But how are we going to catch Frisky?" Rachel asked. "He's still darting around like a pig."

"Or being chased and cuddled by Jack Frost," said Kirsty.

She pointed to where Jack was sprinting around a frozen fountain after Frisky.

"Come here!" he roared. "Come back! I want a cuddle with you!"

He threw himself across the fountain

and managed to catch Frisky by the
back legs. Frisky neighed and wriggled as
Jack Frost picked him up.

"I've got something for you," Jack Frost
said, panting as he tried to hold on to
Frisky.

He pointed over to a small iron bench.
The fairies were startled to see a large
soft toy in the shape of Jack Frost. It was
sitting on the bench with its legs crossed
and a mean expression on its face.

Jack Frost clutched Frisky to his chest and carried him over to the toy. He put him down at the toy's feet.

"There," he said. "Isn't it the most beautiful thing you've ever seen?"

Frisky oinked like a pig and shrank back from Jack Frost.

"I don't think he's very impressed," said Rachel.

"Jack Frost doesn't know anything about what foals really like," Kirsty said. "He has no idea how to look after one properly."

"But Frisky isn't acting like a foal," said Rachel in a thoughtful voice. "He's acting like a pig. Treating him like a foal won't do any good. We have to think of something a pig would want – like acorns."

"You're right," said Penelope.

She waved her wand, and a big basket of acorns appeared on the ground below. While Jack Frost was still trying to get Frisky to play with the soft toy, the three fairies zoomed downwards and hid behind a nearby hay bale.

Kirsty watched Frisky as he stared at the acorns.

"Come on," she whispered, hardly daring to breathe in case it frightened him away. "Come on, Frisky."

Frisky took one step towards them... and then another. Then he trotted over to the acorns and started nibbling. But Jack Frost was close behind him. The Ice Lord scooped Frisky up into his arms and squeezed him tightly.

"I've got another surprise for you," he

bellowed at the little foal.

"Oh poor Frisky," said Penelope.

Jack Frost lifted Frisky's ear and whispered into it, "I've built you a new home."

He strode away from the acorn basket, carrying Frisky. The three fairies darted high into the air and followed him as he tramped away from the Ice Castle. He walked past frozen fountains and snow-covered shrubs until he reached a little huddle of weeping willows, stiff with frost.

"Close your eyes," Jack
Frost told Frisky.

Frisky oinked
again, his eyes
wide open.
Jack Frost
waved his
wand, and
the weeping
willows
parted their
branches like
curtains. Inside,
the girls saw a foal-sized version of the
Ice Castle. It was guarded by tiny goblin
statues, and Jack Frost clapped his hands
together in delight.

"It looks cleaner and tidier than the
real thing," Rachel whispered.

The windows sparkled, and when
they peered through, the fairies could
see that the little castle looked dry and
bright. There were blue curtains at every
window and the wooden drawbridge had
been polished until it gleamed.

49

"Welcome to your new home," said Jack Frost. "The drawbridge really works."

He put Frisky down and watched him run into the castle. Then he closed the drawbridge, and the fairies heard a furious oink from the little foal. The next moment, Frisky came sailing over the castle wall and began to snuffle at the ground like a pig looking for food.

"Frisky, stop!" Jack Frost roared.

Kirsty turned to Rachel and Penelope with an excited look on her face. Seeing Frisky snuffling like a pig had given her an idea.

"I've got a plan," she whispered. "I think I know how we can get Frisky back."

A Spell and a Splash

As quickly as she could, Kirsty explained her plan. Frisky had to be treated like a pig, if he was going to relax enough to let anyone near him. As soon as they heard the plan, Rachel and Penelope started to smile.

"Good thinking, Kirsty," Rachel said.

Penelope raised her wand and spoke the words of a spell.

"Frisky thinks that he's a pig.
We'll lay a trail of acorns big!
Then find a game for a foal to enjoy,
And he'll be such a happy boy!"

Instantly, a trail of golden fairy dust whooshed out of the wand tip and swirled across the garden to an open lawn. There it  hopped across the grass, laying a trail of acorns wherever it touched the ground. At the far end of the lawn was a slope

leading to a big, muddy ditch. Kirsty and
Rachel smiled.

"That's perfect for Frisky," said Rachel.

Frisky spotted the acorns at once and
oinked with delight. He rushed towards
them, snuffling, and started to gobble
them up. Jack Frost stumbled after him,
waving his arms and shouting. Frisky
took absolutely no notice. He was having
a wonderful time.

Jack Frost kept on running, trying to catch the little foal. Penelope, Rachel and Kirsty fluttered above the last acorn.

"Get ready to catch Frisky as soon as he reaches us," said Kirsty.

The foal snuffled up the last acorn and the fairies zoomed down to catch him. But Jack Frost was close behind, and he flew through the air, snatching Frisky and splashing down into the muddy ditch below. SPLOOSH! Mucky water shot

into the air
and drenched
the fairies'
delicate wings,
bringing them all
tumbling down
into the ditch.
Frisky squirmed
away from Jack
Frost as the fairies started to wade out of
the ditch, shaking mud from their wings.

"Frisky, it's me," Penelope said.

Frisky looked confused, and tried to run
away. But his little hooves slipped in the
mud and he slid sideways, knocking all
the fairies over again. Jack Frost scrabbled
towards him. Then he slipped and fell flat
on his face in the mud.

"This way, Frisky!" Kirsty said.

"Over here," Jack Frost called, wiping mud from his eyes.

The foal darted sideways and the Ice Lord managed to catch him. But Frisky squirmed away again, sending a spray of mud into Jack Frost's open mouth. As he spluttered, Frisky ran into the waiting arms of Kirsty and Rachel.

Penelope flew to the magical foal's

side and gave
him a gentle
cuddle. He gave
a little snorting
noise and snuggled
closer to her. He
snuffled…and
then he let out
a loud, horsey
NEIGH.

Rachel, Kirsty and Penelope
exchanged delighted smiles as Frisky
whinnied in delight.

"He's back to being a proper foal," said
Rachel. "Thank goodness."

"Now we just have to persuade him to
get out of the mud," said Penelope with
a laugh.

"Let's get *ourselves* out of the mud

first," said Kirsty, gazing down at her mucky jeans and T-shirt. "It's lucky we were wearing our oldest clothes."

Laughing, they helped each other out of the mud, holding on to Frisky to make sure that he didn't scamper off again. Then Penelope waved her wand and instantly their clothes were clean and dry once more.

"Aren't you forgetting someone?" Jack Frost hissed, crawling out of the ditch on his hands and knees.

"This is all your fault."

His clothes were soaked. His spiky hair was

dripping with globules of mud. Even his eyelids had mud on them. He stood up and glared at Penelope.

"Give him back to me," he demanded.

"You know I'm not going to do that," said Penelope in her gentle voice.

"I've lost the duckling, the lamb and now the foal," Jack Frost wailed. "What am I going to do for a petting farm now?"

"They weren't yours to begin with," said Kirsty.

"It's not fair," Jack Frost complained, slumping down on to the grass. "Everyone's so mean to me. No one wants me."

Just then, Rachel noticed something moving out of the corner of her eye. She turned and saw that Snowdrop and the snow goose had followed Jack Frost as fast as their little legs could carry them. Now they were gazing at him with longing expressions.

"It's not true that no one wants you," Rachel said. "You're just not looking in the right place."

But Jack Frost wasn't in the mood to listen. He got up and stomped away with a grumpy expression. The snow geese followed him, and the girls sighed.

"I hope that he starts paying attention to them again soon," said Kirsty. "I want them to be happy, just like Penelope and Frisky."

"As soon as the magical farm babies are back where they belong, I'm sure Jack Frost will notice the snow geese again," said Penelope.

"That's another good reason to find the last of the missing animals," said Rachel. "Everyone should be with their pets, just like you and Frisky."

True Friends

Penelope smiled at Frisky. He was still rolling around in the ditch.

"Things are starting to get back to normal," she said. "Now I need to take Frisky back to the Fluttering Fairyland Farm."

"Farmer Francis will be so glad to see him," said Kirsty.

"He'll be very happy," said Penelope. "But before I can return him, I need to take you two back to Greenfields Farm."

She held out her arms, and Rachel and Kirsty shared a hug with her.

"Thank you for helping me to find Frisky," she said. "Thank you with all my heart."

"We're so happy to be able to help you and the other Baby Farm Animal Fairies," said Rachel.

Penelope smiled and raised her wand. Everything around Rachel and Kirsty seemed to shimmer and blur. Then they were surrounded by lush green grass. The four horses in the paddock were still there. But the foals were no longer rolling around in the squishy mud, squealing and snorting like piglets – they were back

in the paddock where they belonged,
frisking around. The horses looked on as
the little foals played together.

"Well, they seem to be having lots of
fun," said Kirsty, laughing.

"It's so good to see them back to normal again," said Rachel.

"Yes," Kirsty agreed. "But they do look rather grubby. Let's bath and groom them ready for the photo shoot."

The girls hurried back to the gate and collected their buckets of soapy water. Then they caught the playful foals and washed each

one nice and clean before brushing their coats and manes until they gleamed.

"Now we have to get their photos

taken before they get dirty again," said
Rachel, clipping a halter around each
foal's neck.

"Harriet said that they would wait for
us in the barn," said Kirsty, gathering up
the grooming equipment.

They hurried to the barn, and found
Blossom still standing outside. She gave
a loud moo as she watched the girls lead
the foals into the barn. Harriet and Niall
were inside setting up a camera on a
tripod.

"We've made a lovely play area for
them," said Niall when he saw the girls.
"Wow, they have never looked cleaner.
Come on, foals."

Harriet and Niall took lots of photos
for the website and posters as the little
foals played and frisked around together.

Rachel and Kirsty watched the photo shoot, and even Blossom wandered in to find out what was going on.

In the farmhouse that evening, the girls sat down around the kitchen table with Mr and Mrs Tate. Harriet and Niall were holding the new poster between them.

"I can't wait to see it," said Rachel, squeezing her best friend's hand.

Smiling, Harriet and Niall laid the new poster out on the table. Everyone smiled at the funny photos of the foals.

"It's perfect," said Mr Tate. "The poster looks great and the photos will bring visitors flocking to the farm."

"The girls did a wonderful job of grooming the foals," said Harriet. "One of them is so clean that it's almost as if it's sparkling."

Kirsty and Rachel leaned over and looked closer at the picture.

"The foal *is*

71

sparkling," Kirsty whispered in Rachel's ear. "It's *Frisky*. How did he get on the poster?"

"It must be fairy magic," Rachel replied.

It was good to know that Frisky was safe. But they also knew that they couldn't relax yet. Their fairy friends still had to get one more magical baby farm animal back.

"Billie can trust us to help bring Chompy home," said Kirsty. "We won't let Jack Frost turn tomorrow's

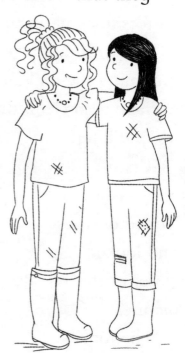

grand opening into a disaster."

The girls exchanged a secret smile.

"You're right," said Rachel. "The Baby Farm Animal Fairies can depend on us — and so can Greenfields Farm!"

The End

**Now it's time for Kirsty and
Rachel to help ...**

Billie the Baby Goat Fairy

Read on for a sneak peek ...

The sun was shining brightly on
Greenfields Farm, and the fresh early-
morning breeze made it the perfect
spring day. Butterflies and bees were
already busy around the flowers and
bushes. Kirsty Tate and her best friend
Rachel Walker were walking away from
the farmhouse, feeling a very special kind
of excitement.

"The big day has finally arrived,"
said Kirsty, pausing to take a long, deep
breath of fresh country air. "I can't wait
for the grand opening to start!"

The girls – together with Kirsty's

parents – had been staying at the farm during spring half term to help the Tates' friends, Harriet and Niall Hawkins, get the farm ready to welcome visitors.

"I want to be sure that everything is perfect," said Rachel.

The girls had been given the very special job of looking after the baby farm animals. They had loved every minute of it, and this morning they had woken up extra early so that they could check on all the baby animals before the grand opening.

"Let's visit the ducklings first," said Kirsty.

They walked past the barn and along the winding path that led to the duck pond. As soon as they had walked between the trees, they saw the glittering water of the pond, with its tall reeds and its happy ducks. Lots of little ducklings were quacking as they splashed around.

"They all look fine," said Rachel. "Shall we check the lambs next? I love the way they bounce around when they see us. It's as if they've got springs in their hooves."

Read **Billie the Baby Goat Fairy** to find out what adventures are in store for Kirsty and Rachel!

Competition!

The Baby Animal Farm Fairies have created
a special competition just for you!

Collect all four books in the Baby Animal Farm series
and answer the special questions in the back of each one.

**The horses at
Greenfields Farm
live in a**

_ _ _ _ _ _ _

Once you have all four answers, take the first letter from
each one and arrange them to spell a secret word!
When you have the answer, go online and enter!

We will put all the correct entries into a draw and select
a winner to receive a special Rainbow Magic Goody Bag
featuring lots of treats for you and your fairy friends.
The winner will also feature in a new Rainbow Magic story!

Enter online now at www.rainbowmagicbooks.co.uk

No purchase required. Only one entry per child.
One prize draw will take place on 30/06/2017 and two winners will be chosen.
Alternatively UK readers can send the answer on a postcard to: Rainbow Magic,
The Baby Animal Farm Fairies Competition, Orchard Books, Carmelite House,
50 Victoria Embankment, London, EC4Y 0DZ.
Australian readers can write to: Rainbow Magic, The Baby Animal Farm Fairies Competition,
Hachette Children's Books, Level 17/207 Kent St, Sydney, NSW 2000.
E-mail: childrens.books@hachette.com.au.
New Zealand readers should write to: Rainbow Magic, The Baby Animal Farm
Fairies Competition, PO Box 3255, Shortland St, Auckland 1140

Calling all parents, carers and teachers!
The Rainbow Magic fairies are here to help
your child enter the magical world of reading.
Whatever reading stage they are at, there's
a Rainbow Magic book for everyone!
Here is Lydia the Reading Fairy's guide to
supporting your child's journey at all levels.

Starting Out

Our Rainbow Magic Beginner Readers are perfect for first-time readers who are just beginning to develop reading skills and confidence. Approved by teachers, they contain a full range of educational levelling, as well as lively full-colour illustrations.

Developing Readers

Rainbow Magic Early Readers contain longer stories and wider vocabulary for building stamina and growing confidence. These are adaptations of our most popular Rainbow Magic stories, specially developed for younger readers in conjunction with an Early Years reading consultant, with full-colour illustrations.

Going Solo

The Rainbow Magic chapter books - a mixture of series and one-off specials - contain accessible writing to encourage your child to venture into reading independently. These highly collectible and much-loved magical stories inspire a love of reading to last a lifetime.

www.rainbowmagicbooks.co.uk

"Rainbow Magic got my daughter reading chapter books. Great sparkly covers, cute fairies and traditional stories full of magic that she found impossible to put down" - Mother of Edie (6 years)

"Florence LOVES the Rainbow Magic books. She really enjoys readin - Mother of Florence (6 years)

The Rainbow Magic Reading Challenge

Well done, fairy friend – you have completed the book!
This book was worth 5 points.

See how far you have climbed on the
Reading Rainbow opposite.

The more books you read, the more points you will get,
and the closer you will be to becoming a Fairy Princess!

How to get your Reading Rainbow
1. Cut out the coin below
2. Go to the Rainbow Magic website
3. Download and print out your poster
4. Add your coin and climb up the Reading Rainbow!

There's all this and lots more at
www.rainbowmagicbooks.co.uk

You'll find activities, competitions, stories, a special
newsletter and complete profiles of all the
Rainbow Magic fairies. Find a fairy with your name!